# StormWrangler

## COERT VOORHEES

### illustrated by Mike Guillory

bright sky press
HOUSTON, TEXAS

# StormWrangler

## Coert Voorhees

### Illustrated by Mike Guillory

For George and William Nelson

Yeahaw!

*[signatures]*

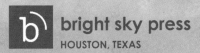

bright sky press
HOUSTON, TEXAS

Well, howdy there, pardner!
Storm Wrangler's the name.
Saddle up, and I'll show you:
tamin' weather's the game.

If gusts blow and bluster,
and fright comes a-crawlin',
be aware: it ain't wind,
that's just me a-yee-hawin'!

I've conquered nor'easters
and thunderhead squalls.
From drizzle to deluge,
boy, I've seen it all.

Tornadoes in Kansas
that thrashed on the land.
They whipped and they wriggled
like snakes in headstands.

And out in the ocean
a beast spanned the sky.
The hurricane Cyclops,
no wind in his eye.

You'll love wrasslin' monsters.
No need to hide, youngster!
These earmuffs will block out
the rumble of thunder.

When bolts zap and crackle
way out in the field,
gear up for the scuffle
with your lightning shield.

But what about rainfall?
And snow, sleet, and hail?
You've got to have somethin'
to withstand the gale.

So whip out your jacket
to clash with the banshee.
Complete with a hood
if that cyclone gets nasty.

Come wrangle with me, friend,
and make yourself proud.
A tempest's a brewin'.
You'll see by the clouds.

Flared eyes of an ogre,
great billowing head.
Cool breath, it's a whirlwind!
The air fills with dread.

Not wispy like cirrus.
Not stacked high like stratus.
That cumulus varmint
is comin' right at us.

Now, hood on! And shield up!
Sling your lasso with pride.
'Cause ropin' a twister's
one heck of a ride!

The best part comes after,
I promise, you'll learn.
The air crisp and sparkling,
bright calmness returns.

The sun always comes out
no matter the storm.
Plumb beat, yet victorious,
we'll watch it transform.

This here's why I wrangle,
for views such as these.
My boots up, my hat off,
some mint in my tea.

They call us Storm Wranglers,
Side-by-side through it all.
Brave, strong, & courageous.
Now let's hear that "Yee-haw!"

# Weather Terms

A **gust** is a sudden, strong rush of air, with variations of 10 knots or more between peaks and lulls.

**Drizzle** is a fine misty rain consisting of numerous minute droplets of water less than 0.5 mm in diameter.

A **deluge** is a great and overwhelming flood of water, or a large and heavy rainfall.

A **thunderhead** is a round mass of cumulus clouds that appears before a thunderstorm.

A **squall** is a brief and violent windstorm also consisting of rain or snow.

A **nor'easter** is a strong low-pressure system that affects the Mid Atlantic and New England States. It can form over land or the coastal waters. These winter weather events produce heavy snow, rain, and tremendous waves that crash onto Atlantic beaches. Wind gusts can exceed hurricane force in intensity. These storms get their name from the continuously strong northeasterly winds blowing in from the ocean ahead of the storm and over the coastal areas.

A **tornado** is a violently whirling column of air seen as a funnel-shaped cloud that usually destroys everything in its narrow path.

A **hurricane** is a violent tropical cyclone that produces extreme winds and rain.

**Thunder** is a sound that is caused by the rapidly expanding gases in a lightning discharge.

A **lightning bolt** is a visible electrical discharge produced by a thunderstorm.

**Sleet** is pellets of ice composed of frozen or mostly frozen raindrops or refrozen partially melted snowflakes. These pellets of ice usually bounce after hitting the ground or other hard surfaces.

**Hail** is showery precipitation in the form of irregular pellets or balls of ice more than 5 mm in diameter, falling from a cumulonimbus cloud.

A **gale** is an extra tropical low or an area of sustained surface winds of 39 mph to 54 mph.

A **cyclone** is a storm with strong winds rotating around a center of low pressure, in the United States it is also used as another word for tornado and in the Indian Ocean area it is used to describe a hurricane.

A **tempest** is a violent storm with high winds and is usually accompanied by rain; it is similar to a squall.

**Cirrus clouds** are high-level clouds (16,000 feet or higher), composed of ice crystals and appearing in the form of white, delicate filaments or white or mostly white patches or narrow bands.

A **stratus cloud** is a low, generally gray cloud layer with a fairly uniform base. Stratus may appear in the form of ragged patches, but otherwise does not exhibit individual cloud elements as do cumulus and stratocumulus clouds. Fog usually is a surface-based form of stratus.

**Cumulus clouds** are white billowy clouds with a dark flat base.

**Twister** is another name for tornado.

A **whirlwind** is a small rotating windstorm of limited extent.